Max showed his lost tooth to h

who was also his next-door neighbor.

"Cool!" Amy said. "Put it under your pillow."

Max said, "Um... I don't think so."

Amy looked surprised. "Don't you want the Tooth Fairy to come and leave you money?"

Max rolled his eyes. "Nah, I don't believe in the Tooth Fairy." Then, instead of putting his tooth under his pillow, Max tossed it into the wastebasket!

The next day, Max woke early and checked under his pillow. Of course, there was nothing there.

"Told you," Max said to Amy.

Amy frowned. "Hmm," she said, "maybe the Tooth Fairy just couldn't find your tooth."

As Max stood up, he tripped over the wastebasket. Out rolled a coin!

"That's just a coincidence," he said. "Someone must have dropped that coin in there by mistake or something."

"But," Amy said, picking up the coin, "then where's your tooth?"

Max wasn't sure what to believe. So, the next time he lost a tooth, he hid it where he was sure no one would think to look—under the dog's water bowl!

"This is a test," he said to himself. "If the Tooth Fairy can find my tooth, I might believe she's real. If not, there's definitely no such thing."

This is sooo not funny.
SLURP
SLURP
SLURP
SLURP
Doggy

In the morning, Max was shocked to discover a puddle in the middle of the floor and a coin under the dog's water bowl. *Maybe there is a Tooth Fairy after all,* he thought. Or, maybe someone dropped some change and then accidentally put the bowl on top of it.

"No," Max convinced himself, "this proves nothing."

A month later, Max had another loose tooth. This time he was determined to prove, once and for all, that there was no Tooth Fairy. When the tooth came out, Max called Amy and had her come over to watch as he locked the tooth in his safe—the one to which only he had the combination.

"She'll never find it in there," he said.

He thinks he's Sooo Smart.
click
click
click
click
click
click
click
click
click
click
click
click
click
click
click
click
click
click
click

The next day, Max couldn't believe his eyes. He called Amy over immediately.

"She found it in the safe? Wow! She's good," Amy said.

"But this doesn't make sense," Max said. Then he snapped his fingers.

"I've got it!" he said. "I know what I've been doing wrong."

“Give it up,” Amy said. “She’s real!”

“No, every tooth was hidden in the house,” Max explained. “This one,” he added, showing Amy the latest tooth he’d lost, “I’m burying under the old oak tree outside. She’ll never find it there!”

1
2
3
4
5

In the morning, Max and Amy stared down the hole beside the tree. Buried there was ANOTHER coin—and no tooth. But this time, there was something else, too.

"Hey," Amy said. "There's a note."

Max's jaw dropped.

"And it's from the Tooth Fairy!" Amy yelled.

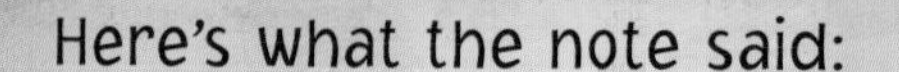

Here's what the note said:

Dear Max,

This has been loads of fun, but I hope you have a little more faith in me now. I have left you a special pillow in your room. Please use it from now on, and I promise there will always be a surprise left for you in the morning! (By the way, keep up the brushing. Your teeth look great!)

Love,

The Tooth Fairy

From that day forward, Max always left his teeth right where the Tooth Fairy had told him to leave them. And he never tested the Tooth Fairy again!